ZOE'S JUNGLE

By Bethanie Deeney Murguia

ARTHUR A. LEVINE BOOKS

An Imprint of Scholastic Inc.

Text and art copyright © 2014 by Bethanie Deeney Murguia. · All rights reserved. Published by Arthur A. Levine Books, an imprint of Scholastic Inc., *Publishers since 1920*. SCHOLASTIC and the LANTERN LOGO are trademarks and/or registered trademarks of Scholastic Inc. No part of this publication may be reproduced, stored in a retrieval system, or transmitted in any form or by any means, electronic, mechanical, photocopying, recording, or otherwise, without written permission of the publisher. For information regarding permission, write to Scholastic Inc., Attention: Permissions Department, 557 Broadway, New York, NY 10012. Library of Congress Cataloging-in-Publication Data · Murguia, Bethanie Deeney, author, illustrator. Zoe's jungle / by Bethanie Deeney Murguia — First edition. pages cm Summary: As their mother counts down the time, Zoe and her sister Addie hurry to complete their game of chase in an imaginary jungle. · ISBN 978-0-545-55869-3 (alk. paper) — ISBN 978-0-545-55870-9 (ebook) 1. Imagination—Juvenile fiction. 2. Play—Juvenile fiction. 3. Sisters—Juvenile fiction. [1. Imagination—Fiction. 2. Play—Fiction. 3. Sisters—Fiction.] I. Title. PZ7.M944Zon 2014 · 813.6—dc23 2013039059 · 10 9 8 7 6 5 4 3 2 1   14 15 16 17 18 · Printed in China   38 First edition, June 2014 · The artwork was created in pen-and-ink and watercolor. The text was set in Chaloops Regular. Book design by Chelsea C. Donaldson.

For the Little Monkeys

—B.D.M.

High above the jungle floor,

the fearless explorer glimpses

a rare spotted Addiebeast.

She sails through the treetops,

quickly closing in on the elusive creature.

It's still adventure time!

And exploring time!

It is definitely NOT leaving time!

I repeat, it is NOT . . ."

Four minutes!

"Is there no respect for
the explorer and her quest?"

"Come on!" says Addie.

"We can still play chase."

The wild Addiebeast disappears into the jungle.

The clever explorer is hot on the trail.
No human has ever come so close to
catching this strange animal.

This is a tremendous opportunity,
a career-defining mission.

The brave explorer dashes across
the river shortcut.
The wild Addiebeast is just ahead.

There is no time to waste.

Think like the beast.

The stealthy explorer sneaks through the dense underbrush.

The wild Addiebeast is only a few steps away.

A lifetime of preparation

comes down to this moment.

The relentless explorer
chases the wild Addiebeast
to its treetop lair.

This is a great moment in the history of everything.

Quiet. No sudden movements.

And the Addiebeast has been captured! Has the world ever witnessed such a remarkable feat, such a display of strength, ingenuity, and persistence? This amazing story will be remembered until the end of time, maybe longer. It is truly unfathomable in its —

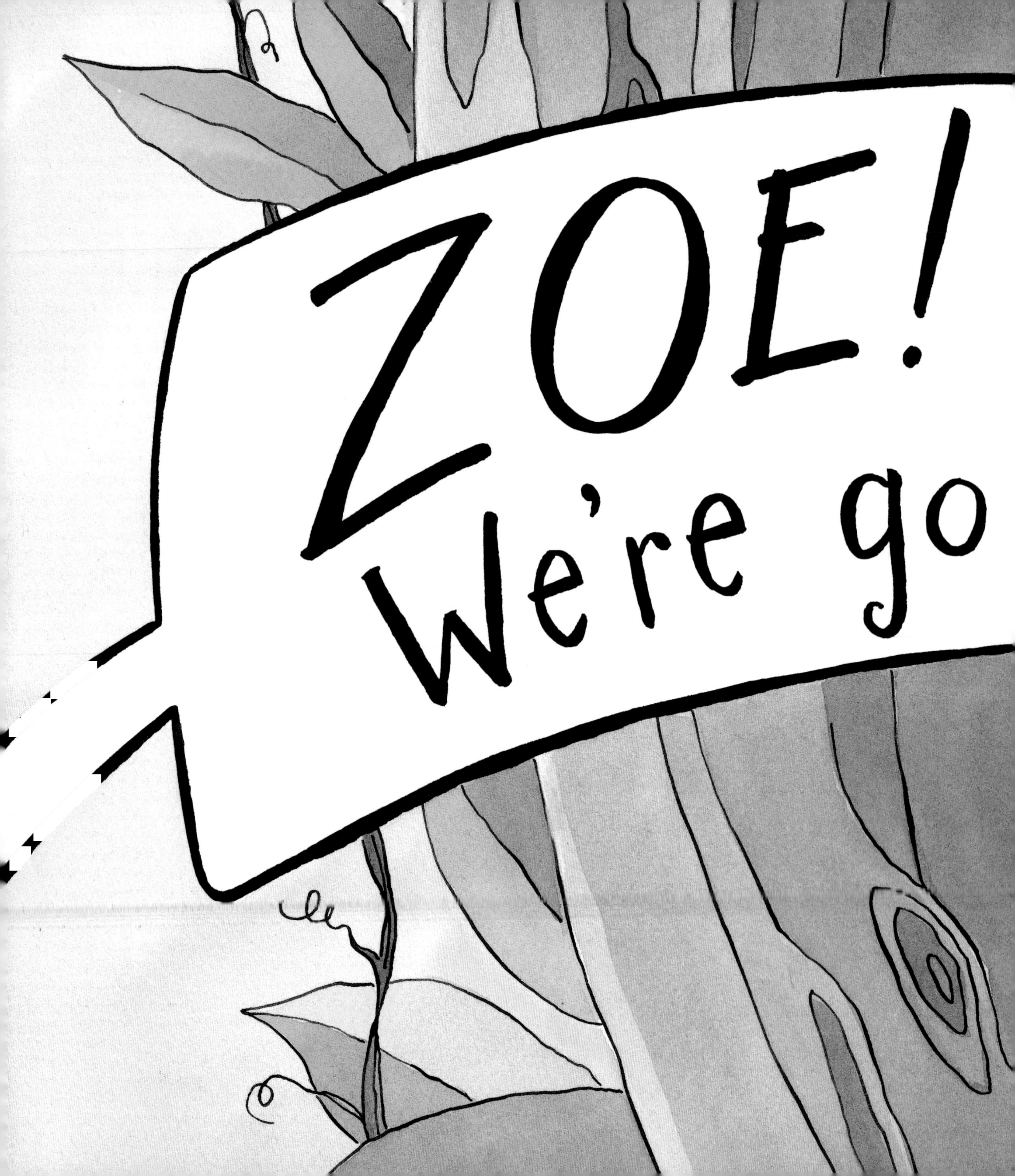
ZOE!
We're go

"Come on, Addie.

It's not chase time anymore.

It's the best time of all . . ."

"Story time!

Today, *I* have a great one.

It all begins with a fearless explorer . . ."